Written by
PAUL MANNING

Illustrated by
NICOLA BAYLEY

WALKER BOOKS
LONDON

Who's that
in the big
white
hat?

What shall
we make—
a chocolate
cake?

Three, four...
a spoonful
more.

Slop,
splatter,
mix the
batter.

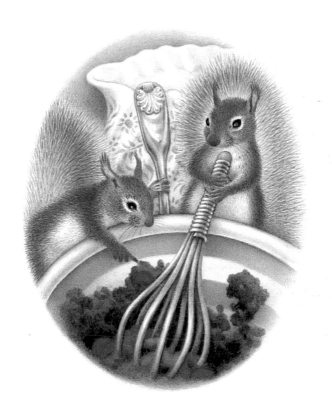

Sticky paste,
try a taste.

Cook looking,
how's it
cooking?

Bang, bong,
sound the
gong.

What's
for tea?
Look
and see!